The Last Tribune

Matthew P. Schmidt

O&H Books

O and H Books LLC

Contents

To St. Irenaeus, for reasons that will soon be obvious.

The Decision

They said we could destroy entire cities. That one of us, alone, was a match for conventional armies. There was no need for a nation to have more than a handful, for we could fight a whole war by ourselves. But the Old Nations were greedy, bloodthirsty, blood-mad, and built entire legions of us. Until the day they went to war.

Now we knew better, I learned. "We" as in humanity, not just those such as myself. No more elections that would be contested in blood. No more thrones to fight over. Just the United Tribes and, ourselves, their Tribunes. We had even moved beyond the bad old days. Now we fought in simulations, made real by our implants. Only the Final Battle was still fought to the death.

We watched it in the school auditorium, all classes canceled. For six hours we watched the battle progress, the Blue-Gold Tribune leveling building after building in search of the Violet Tribune. I had seen glimpses of the earlier rounds, and could vaguely remember the finals of '15, when I was seven. But I could not turn my eyes away, as the world's fate hung in balance.

We watched it in silence. The talking heads, present in earlier matches, had shut up. All we saw was the feed from the aerial camera drones that swarmed at a distance, watching to see who would make the Final Decision.

For six hours we watched until we saw a man die.

The Blue-Gold Tribune blasted a building to bits, the debris falling everywhere. One large chunk slammed into his defensive fields and he momentarily staggered. The Violet Tribune swooped an impossible banking curve around the rubble and fired his power rifle into our champion. The otherworldly energy knocked him back. He fell, rolled, stopped. We all gasped.

The Violet Tribune drew a curved sword with a shining-bright edge and sliced his head off.

We all roared, fear and despair and celebration and anger all at once.

The drones circled closer, but our champion was clearly dead. In the distance, violet fireworks boomed. "And that's it for the Final Battle of '20," said the reporter, a Violet by his looks and commentary. "What an amazing performance by both of them, well fought..."

Well fought? I wanted to argue, to shout "Cheap trick!" or "It wasn't his fault the rubble hit him!", and others did. But I was silent as the teachers yelled at us.

After all, this was the price we paid for peace. No matter who won the Final Battle, or how, we would serve his choice without question. And so we watched in silence again as the camera cut to the Tribal Conclave, where the Violet Tribune arrived to the celebration of the Violet Government. We watched as the Supreme Iudices asked for any who would challenge his victory, and no Tribe did. They declared him the Victorious Tribune, placed the emerald Laurel on his violet helm. He walked up to the podium in the Chamber of Decision, the whole world watching.

And with swift motions he signed the Final Ballot, the paper that gave the Violet Governor, Junette O'Hara, the mantle of Supreme Consul, and with it, near-absolute power.

The Blue-Golds and kids from allied tribes in the class left, refusing to look at their Violet and Violet Caucus peers. But I sat in thought.

I wasn't old enough yet, but in five years I would be. I had just as many nanobots in my blood, an equal number of hearts, and the same neurojack in my spine. All I needed was the wetware and a power suit and I—*I*—would be the Victorious Tribune in '25.

Of course, I couldn't tell anyone about my newfound resolve. That I even had the neurojack was secret. And children are good at keeping secrets.

I still nearly leaked it once or twice. My parents were careful. A Tribune whose identity was known was of no use to the Tribe. No sleepovers, no community pools, and never talk about the special training. I still went to public school, and had normal friends, and told them my parents were into martial arts.

The next day they published the identities of all 23 Tribunes, including our late champion. He looked like any other teenager, with a causal smile, but an edge in his eyes.

The Victorious Tribune was dead serious in the profile image, and didn't talk to the press the next day. It wasn't as if he had to do anything else for the rest of his life.

"Nah," Melody, my one Violet friend, said. "He's probably just freaking out that he killed someone. Just because you're a Tribune doesn't make it any easier."

"What would you do if you were a Tribune?" I asked.

"Kill the other guy," she said without hesitation. "That'd be my job. You?"

I momentarily lost my train of thought. "I... I would also do my job."

We sat next to each other on the hill near the playground. The other kids, both Blue-Gold and Violet, gave us upset glances. But I didn't pay attention.

I was old enough to start noticing girls, and Melody was, well... She was the prettiest girl I knew, with a perfectly balanced face and curly brown hair. But I had known her since early childhood.

The thought seized me: if I really became the Blue-Gold Tribune, could I still be friends with Melody? No use worrying about it now, I decided. Some of the special training was on mental discipline and stoicism, something that I found I easily grasped.

"Anyway, nothing to worry about," Melody said. "It's not like either of us will ever have to make that choice."

"Right," I lied.

Things got serious when I was thirteen. My parents brought me to Chicago to sign the papers that would retroactively give permission for the fetal implantation surgeries. Their signature was not enough—a Tribune must be entirely willing.

I'll admit I had second thoughts when it was no longer hypothetical. I watched, awed and unnerved, out the aircar's window as we flew, landing on one of the many landing pads of the Tribal Capitol. The tall building—the tallest in the city—was covered with the blue and gold spiral that was our Tribe's emblem.

They were waiting for us—for me. The men hurried us into the building, and then through elevators into a vast waiting room. I saw other families with children my age, but we didn't make eye contact. For every power suit, there could only be one Tribune, after all, and I would only fit one power suit.

"Irenaeus Atticus Gaius," a bored receptionist announced, and my parents hurried me through the doors.

The Tribal Officer was a massive man, terrifying to a kid like me. He asked questions and I gave quiet answers. Was I staying healthy? Keeping up with the training? Good grades? Not getting in trouble? I stammered, because what would they do if I *wasn't* worthy?

Then he got quiet, too. "Young man, do you understand the weight of responsibility that will fall on you?"

"Yes, sir," I said.

"If you are selected to be a Tribune, you will be required to give your life for the Tribe, or take the life of another Tribune."

"I understand, sir."

"Good."

My parents beamed as he handed out paper after paper for us to sign. I was relieved. I had more nanobots in me than human cells at that point, but they needed to start altering my bones once I hit puberty. I had second thoughts, yes, but what the vord was I supposed to do if I didn't want this? Tell them to suck the nanobots out of me? I didn't even bleed red—not that my skin ever broke.

"Remember, young man," the Tribal Officer said. "Your victory is all that matters. The entire Tribe depends on you. So nothing else matters. No sex, no drugs, nothing but pursuit of victory. We all depend on you, every last man, woman, and child."

"I understand, sir," I said.

But, in truth, I didn't.

They took me alone to a back room, where I sat on a chair that was likely hundreds of years old. Like all the Old Technology, it was still in perfect condition. A doctor attached the cord to the neurojack in my spine. My head first felt like someone was massaging it badly it, then pressuring it, then slicing it in two.

I saw double as my two eyes stopped being in sync. The world faded, and I saw lights and colors and explosions like a high-speed dream. Sound chimed in my mind, colors and shapes and heat all as one.

Then it all faded.

I groaned in pain, and a nurse injected something. "You'll feel better in a bit."

As I walked back to my parents, I realized I could see lines of fire without even thinking about it. I could tell that Dad was 181 centimeters tall, and that at our walking speed, we would cross the waiting room in thirteen seconds.

I glanced at a boy and met his eyes. I saw, for a moment, an unidentified contact that had no signs of hostility. He looked into my eyes and looked away immediately.

I couldn't stop thinking about it all the way home.

They had to take me out of public school. Since my physical dimensions were being altered to fit an ancient power suit, it would be pretty obvious who I was.

And the day before I left, as we sat together in our usual spot, I broke down and told her.

"You're kidding me," Melody said, bright blue eyes wide. "You? I... I never..."

"It's no big deal to me," I said. "It's just who I am." But I couldn't help but see and feel with instincts that were not my own, perhaps not even human.

"But..." She took a deep breath, held it in for four seconds, and let it out, like they taught us both in our shared martial arts class. "All right. I'll keep your secret. Promise."

"Promise," I said, wrapping a finger around hers. Puberty was awkward enough without your hands warping to fit an ancient gauntlet. "We'll stay in contact," I said belatedly.

"Of course."

But in truth, we couldn't see each other at all.

The private school they sent me to, the Caesar TCA Academy, was *only* for Tribunes—technically, Tribune Candidate Apprentices. The top graduates would become Tribune Candidates, and the rest...

I didn't dare think of that possibility on the crowded, armored airbus there.

The place looked as foreboding as vord. Dead, cratered grounds surrounded the fortress-like main complex. Air defense systems and radars strutted out from the modern, weak field generators, enough to perhaps slow a rogue Tribune for a minute or two.

One wing was massive and stacked high with windows—dormitories enough for 1,200 Tribune Candidate Apprentices to each have their own tiny room.

"Cell" might be more accurate. I had a mirror, a desk, a bed that I barely fit in, a locker, and a terminal. The terminal had no screen—you had to plug it into your neurojack.

I lay on my bed, exhausted from orientation and being yelled at by an increasingly large number of increasingly angry people. I figured there would be no games, but I could at least call my parents and Melody to tell them I arrived safely.

I took the cord and inserted it with some trepidation. The holographic terminal, invisible to all but myself, appeared in the air. I tapped the comms button.

Only Mom and Dad were listed.

Figured. They wouldn't let me talk to my friends. Well, I could at least tell my parents I had survived my first day.

Calling Octavius Scipio Gaius...

Dad picked up immediately. He couldn't see my face, only me his. "How is it?" Dad asked. "Why no video?"

"They don't have video over here," I said. "Anyway, I made it. I got my own room." It occurred to me at that moment that it was certainly strange that a military academy would not force pupils to have roommates. "It's... weird."

"You'll have to tell us all about it," Mom said. "I'm so proud of you."

I smiled. How bad could it be? Besides, even if I couldn't contact my old friends, I had to be able to make friends with *someone* here.

The first day after orientation, we walked out to bleachers by the training grounds, protected by a shimmering field. Marcellinus Aurelius Caesar, Victorious Tribune of '85, stepped out in a power suit. He looked humanoid at best—bright blue and gold with the Tribal Emblem on his chest plate, a nanowoven form-fitting suit with hard plates made of materials we still couldn't reconstruct, jets and weapon belts and a helm without eyes or visor. "I am wearing the Eagle VIa. You will fight in this or one of our Tribe's other suits," he boomed, his voice amplified by the power suit. "You will be, for the most part, invincible. Fire!"

One of the school's gravtanks fired. He dodged with inhuman reflexes and speed, then leaped into the air with his jets. He swung his arm laser and sliced the gravtank in two.

Another fired at him, and he did not dodge. It exploded against his shining fields, leaving him unharmed. When he landed, you couldn't even tell. "There is one weapon that even a power suit cannot stop, and that is the Misericord." He unsheathed a blade with a star-bright edge and cut into his gauntlet. It left a mark.

"There are two, and only two, ways to kill a man in a power suit. One, hit the vorder with enough force that you damage his internal organs beyond his self repair systems. Two, get in close and slice him up. You will never assume Way One has succeeded until our Tribe's fireworks blast. And you will never attempt Way Two unless you are absolutely sure you have disabled the other vorder.

"Kids, you're here for one, and only one, reason. To kill that other vorder. If you spend a millisecond on anything that does not help you win, I will kill you myself. Questions?"

We had none.

We ate in a cavernous mess hall, which, as massive as it was, could not feed all of us at once. There were four meal periods depending on what classes you were in, or so I naively thought. It still occurred to me as strange that we didn't seem to be arranged in houses or teams or however the vord we were supposed to do this.

You had to eat exactly your ration, no matter how unappetizing it was, watched by the camera bulbs in every corner. You could not barter with the more edible portions. Seating was equally strict, assigned by the robots.

I found Seat 45-A and sat down, waiting for the signal to start. In the distance, a kid prayed over his food, only to be mocked by his randomly assigned peers, and a teacher shouted at all of them to shut up.

"Eat!" came the order.

We ate. I sat across from a kid who looked very much like me. In fact, he had an identical build. "Eagle VIa?" I asked.

"Yes," he said, startled. "I'm... I'm Cletus. Student #0234."

"Irenaeus. #0625."

We shook almost identical hands, his skin just slightly darker.

"I'm a Golem II," a bulky kid said. "Severian. #0124."

"Priscilla," said the remaining member of our table, a young razor-thin woman, as newly bald as the rest of us. "I pilot a Harpy. #0006."

"Which one?" Cletus asked. "And you don't 'pilot' a power suit."

She scowled. "I don't know. My mom just sent me here."

"You don't just *become* a Tribune Candidate Apprentice," I said, offended.

"Yeah, well, when your mom's a Tribal Official and you were born seventeen years before the Tribal Conclave, you don't get a choice."

"Sure, *princess*," Severian said.

"Fatso."

"It's muscle, not fat."

"Are we, like, getting callsigns now?" Cletus asked.

Everyone laughed nervously.

"Look, whatever," Severian said. "Unlike *some* people here, my family needs the subsidy. So if anyone vords with me..."

"Hey, hey," I said. "We're all on the same side here. We need to, like, swap techniques or something."

"Maybe we should learn them first?" Priscilla asked icily.

"STOP TALKING!" ordered a staff member. "Eat!"

We shut up and ate.

While we—all the Apprentices for the same power suit—would hypothetically have identical bodies, our neural tissue was just slightly different. The wetware sometimes had errors. So we spent our first few days in half-simulated, half-real systems as technicians swore at us and told us to think of different things.

I couldn't help but get excited, though. We started with the radar and lidar senses, which formed a three-dimensional image like a mix of sight and hearing, but crystal clear. Priscilla said she could hear targets as musical notes, while I just felt them as tones in different colors. The primary target (a.k.a., the enemy Tribune) was a loud red.

Next were the various HUDs, internal sensor readouts, and the like. When the technician flipped the switch, I could suddenly tell the pulse rates of both my hearts.

After that was the verniers—the fancy name for the thrusters built into every power suit. We could also fly by canceling gravity, but that worked instantly for me, so we didn't test it out. The verniers didn't, and every time the technician told me to the thrust to the left the machine said I thrusted to the right. But I got through it.

Weapons followed. The Eagle VIa was not the most loaded of all power suits, but had its own array of miniature nuclear weapons. It also had a megawatt laser, numerous proximity mines and tiny drones, several conventional guns that shot needle-thin flechettes, and, of course, the power rifle. The only thing we didn't test was the Misericord, because those just "worked" apparently.

Finally, a plethora of reflexes had to be tested. The defensive fields were purely autonomic, like breathing, and when they weren't working right, it felt like I was drowning.

In all of this, to be clear, I was just sitting in a chair while the technicians pressed buttons and yelled at me. They wouldn't trust some random kid who still couldn't quite shave with the only remaining Eagle VI.

But, I knew, they were preparing me for the real thing. Or at least a quality simulation of the real thing.

The Perfect City, Neo Babylon, had been duplicated in every aspect, down to the flags of the Old Nations at the UN Capitol that rippled in the simulated wind. Every last street was the same, every last window and display ad, every last groundcar and its accompanying now-meaningless license plate, even the graffiti and grime of the miles of sewer systems. As in the real world, there were no people.

I stood in one street of the perfectly symmetrical city, just as if I was really there. I was really in a chair with my neurojack plugged into one of the simulation supercomputers, but in the virtual world, I wore a power suit—the Eagle VIa.

My expanded senses told me of the whole virtual world around me. Soft blue tones showed simulated camera drones, and louder ones groundcars and other drones. All of it was a lie. But what was not a lie was the red SIM light in the corner of my HUD.

"Do you see the SIM light?" Dante, the teacher, asked me over the virtual radio.

"Yes, sir," I said.

"Remember it. I swear to you, from the depths of my soul, that we will never trick you into thinking something's a simulation when it's not. Because one of these days, for you, it might not be."

"Yes, sir."

"Great. Let's start by blowing geff up. Pick a building."

I looked around and saw a tall apartment complex. My wetware locked on to it.

"Perfect. Now shoot that vorder with your power rifle."

I aimed, pulled the trigger, and an unbelievably bright light struck it, then blasted through it. The building's remains shuddered, fell apart, and completely collapsed.

"Woah," I said.

"Yeah. Good thing we didn't make any more of these, huh? Let's try your laser next."

I sliced through another building until my laser grew hot and it stopped.

"So, tip: you can't keep using your laser, because it just spits out heat. Even the Old Nations couldn't beat thermodynamics, apparently. Next, let's try some ordnance."

Several explosives later, I had leveled the neighborhood.

"The difference between ordnance and your other weapons is that you have a limited amount of the former. Don't waste it on buildings if you can help it. So run north—you'll see some gravtanks."

I charged forwards, eager, running with superhuman speed. The tanks spotted me and fired at me, but I just stood there and watched the rounds explode a meter away from me. I flinched. Then I fired back and blew them to pieces.

"OK, so don't just stand in the line of fire. Try to dodge these next ones."

More tanks appeared. With instincts I didn't know I had, I flanked them as they turned their turrets. They turned them fast and fired, grazing the edge of my field. I fired back and incinerated them.

"Run *and* fire, there you go. Now let's step it up. Try flying."

I jumped and thought through my verniers. I flew off and slammed into a building. I screamed in pain.

"Oh, yeah, the pain settings are at the level they use for the actual Tribunes. Sorry I didn't bring that up."

I regained my breath. "Let me try that again," I said, jumped up, and slammed into the building again.

"Let's focus on things you *can* do first," Dante said. "Your wetware isn't enough—you need training."

"Fine," I said.

We spent the rest of the session hunting down gravtanks and blowing them up.

The four of us sat at our table on the Wednesday of the second week, exhausted. We had lengthy classes besides our sim sessions, as well as physical ed, and even a shooting range.

"This isn't as bad as I thought it would be," Cletus said.

"Don't vording jinx it!" Priscilla said.

We laughed a little. I had new friends, I supposed, although I badly missed Melody and all my other old friends. But we hardly had any time to see each other, other than here, and the staff was always watching. You couldn't even move a chair without their wrath descending upon you.

"Why are we here?" I asked. "I mean, personally."

"Same reason as everyone else," Cletus said. "For the Tribe."

"Nah," Severian said. "Who cares? The chance of one of us actually becoming Tribune is microscopic. But *I* have a reason, unlike the rest of you. We need the money."

"Whatever," Priscilla said. "I never lost at anything in my life, and I'm not going to lose at this."

How could I explain my resolve? "I... I just want to win," I tried.

They laughed. "Good luck," Severian said.

The Academy taught not only fighting, though most of our time we spent in simulations and training. We also had philosophy, politics, and history.

They had no reason to teach anything we would normally learn in school. With our neurojacks, once we were old enough, we could gain access to the datanet with a thought. No, the only things we learned were the things we had to learn *correctly*.

The politics teacher, Professor Maximus, was the meanest teacher I had ever met. Or maybe it just seemed that way, because every so often he would go on a lengthy rant, sometimes verging into one-way shouting matches, about the Violets. I never dared bring up that I had a close Violet friend, even as he launched into lengthy harangues against imaginary Violet interlocutors, as if, unlike us, they weren't quite human.

"What," he demanded that second week, "is keeping us all from living in a religio-communist nightmare?"

"The Fundamental Rights!" we chanted.

"Who is trying to dismantle them even as we speak?"

"Junette O'Hara and the Violet Caucus!" everyone but me chanted. We were loud enough and myself far enough in the back that my non-participation was unnoticed.

"How do we stop them?"

"Killing their vorder!" we chanted. This, at least I could agree with, my feelings for Melody aside.

Satisfied, the aged professor looked around at us. "Can anyone explain why all of you are thirteen?" He pointed at a girl.

"Sir! Because we were born thirteen years ago!"

"That is the most idiotic answer I have ever heard," the professor spat. The girl winced. "You!" he pointed at me.

"Sir! Because only seventeen-year-olds can be Tribune," I said.

"Good." He pointed at another boy. "You, why does that matter? Why don't we have the same Tribunes fight every five years?"

The boy stammered.

"Well? Out with it!"

"B-b-because the old Tribunes would have more experience?"

"YES!" the professor said. "We have lost three Final Battles in a row. We would never win another if the Violets could trot out their same Tribune every five years. No, as long as the Tribunes cycle every five years there is hope for any Tribe. That is the only way to keep the peace."

"Why not make the minimum age older?" asked a girl.

"Because for the ninety-nine point nine percent of you worthless brats that don't make it, you won't have anything to do with the remainder of your meaningless lives if we waited any longer."

"I thought seventeen was draft age for the Old Nations, sir," Priscilla said.

The professor looked briefly dumbfounded that anyone would have the courage to interject. "Yes, for some," he said. "The Old Nations didn't draft power infantry—like you all, they made them that way from birth."

"I have a question, sir," a boy ventured.

"You've already opened your vording mouth to say that. Ask!"

"Why do we fight the Final Battle with real weapons?"

Nearly everyone laughed—except me, and except the professor. The others stopped short when they saw he didn't. "A good question," he said. "Let me ask you one: would you trust a simulation run by the Violet Caucus?"

"No, sir."

"Precisely. And the Violets and their ilk would not trust a simulation run by ourselves. The Supreme Iudices carefully manage the simulations, and every Tribal Conclave there's some new fight on how exactly to simulate the Old Technology. But we agree to it for the sake of peace. But that is *it!* We cannot risk the outcome of the Final Battle on a faulty simulation." He paced around, angered. "You! Why are the battles to the death?"

"No one who would not give his life for his Tribe is worthy of the title of Tribune, sir!" the young man said.

"Yes! If you ever even *think* about giving up, go to the office and check yourself out *now*. If you ask for mercy, if you *give* mercy, you are worse than they are."

He paused, looking around.

"Anyone fit that description? Anyone going to turn yellow? Anyone going to turn the other cheek?"

"No, sir!" we all chanted.

"I can't hear you!"

"NO, SIR!" we all shouted.

"YES! Now you understand."

The bell rang. We hurried out, but I couldn't quite tell how my heart felt about what had happened. All I knew was my primary heart beat at an even 80 BPM.

The last Saturday of the month, we were all called to the auditorium. I looked around at the seats, but couldn't spot a single empty one.

Principal Caesar stood at the podium. "There are 70,431 Tribune Candidate Apprentices in the Blue-Gold Alliance, 17,601 of the Blue-Gold Tribe itself. For once, all 1,200 at this school have somehow made it through the first month.

"That changes now.

"There are 70,431 TCAs, but only 11 Blue-Gold Alliance power suits. We do not have the time or resources to spend on each of you. We will only spend them on the very best.

"You will all enter an elimination league. You have three lives. Each month, we will match you against another student. If you kill him, you keep your life. If you die, you lose a life. If you lose all your lives, we will expel you without question."

Slight murmurs.

"Your first match is today. You will report to the simulation chambers throughout today, or if need be, tomorrow."

The murmurs roared. "But we haven't had a practice match against other humans yet!" a girl cried out.

"That's correct. You will either learn to swim or drown. Dismissed."

I breathed deeply, hoping that in this virtual world my autonomic nervous system would interpret that as a cue to slow my heart down. Or maybe it should speed up.

A blast of energy fired in the distance. He was ready, whoever "he" was. The league standings didn't give a name, only that he was another Eagle VIa pilot.

I fired upwards, too. Then I ran towards his direction. Another burst of energy leveled a building. My wetware tried to locate him.

I peaked out from behind a building. The building exploded. I flew and rolled. Before I could stand he was there.

He stabbed and stabbed and stabbed as I screamed. Then the world faded.

"YOU LOST."

Predator

"**C**'mon, you vorder," I said to myself in the mirror. I had cut myself shaving–not that I had any idea how to do it to begin with. My face still looked horribly unfamiliar, between the wrongly shaped cheekbones and my still-recent baldness. "We can do this."

But of the twelve hundred students, five hundred ninety-nine others were saying the same thing, after losing to equally incompetent peers.

How many would make it to graduation?

No. No, I was a predator. Think of a hungry, apex predator. It doesn't take risks. It minimizes risks and ruthlessly hunts down its prey. Then, when the moment is right, it strikes.

I had made a mistake. I had taken a risk. I couldn't afford to take unnecessary risks.

"I'm a predator," I said to myself. "I *am* a predator." I'd repeat it to myself every night, I decided. Every night, until it was true.

I looked up the league standings. Severian had won his match, and Cletus and Priscilla had not. I didn't want to discuss my match with them, and found I didn't need to worry about that.

They assigned me to a completely different meal time and table.

It all made so much horrible sense now, I thought as I ate with my new, silent and nameless tablemates. The higher-ranked students would inevitably be a target for bullying and sabotage. So the school had designed itself to prevent that. No roommates. Strictly assigned seating. Cameras everywhere. No intra-school comms.

No, this school was one thing and one thing only, a grindstone to sharpen the Tribe's knives. Anything and anyone that did not contribute was systematically eliminated.

I decided to remain calm as Dante walked me through what I had done wrong.

"Forget the movies," he said as I watched the battle play out in the simulation, my present self in it, like I really had died and was now a ghost. "You're mixing up cover and concealment. The building would *conceal* you from infrared by making your image hazy, but it would not *cover* you from a power rifle."

"What would cover me?" I asked.

"Nothing. Your enemy can level all of Neo Babylon and then the sewer system, too. But the underground would keep you safe for a bit. But that's not your goal. Your goal is to kill the other vorder."

"I want to minimize risks in killing the other vorder," I said.

"Now you're thinking. Step one: don't get vording hit. If all else fails, you need to survive longer. In '95, there was a mutual kill in the Final Battle that our guy survived two more minutes than the Yellow-Red Tribune."

"But the goal is still to kill the other vorder."

"You got it. We don't have infinite time, so rather than talk, what would you like to train? The Eagle VI is especially good at two things: maneuvering and flying."

"Give me flying."

"Sure thing. Let's try just going *up.*"

I concentrated and rocketed upwards.

"OK, gentle, you are thinking *way* too hard. You need to control your reactions or you're going to crash into things."

"Yes, sir," I said, and tried to land. I actually managed it.

"Great. Let's try that again."

We had scrimmages every week, sometimes more than one. The first was only a few days after my first loss.

I breathed deeply as I surveyed the virtual world around me, then aimed directly up and fired.

The other vorder paused a moment, then fired off-center. Panicked? Good.

I knew I was facing a Golem II. Though all power suits were maneuverable, the Golem II was more focused on its fields. I would have to use my superior maneuverability to my advantage, but without flying, because at my skill level, that was a risk.

I was a predator. I did not take risks.

Why not take my time? I walked towards his predicted location, conserving my energy. He would–

The building in front of me disintegrated in a blast of energy. My instincts told me to run, to hide behind another building, but my will made me charge into battle.

I sensed the loud red before I saw the shape, a Golem II bizarrely colored Yellow-Red. I fired on instinct. He just stood there until the firepower broke through his defensive fields and knocked him rolling.

I jumped up. Thrusted over the rubble. I landed, barely. Drew my Misericord. And stabbed him to death.

"YOU WON" the simulation said, and as it faded, I gasped for relief. Seat covered my whole body.

No, though I had won, I had taken an unnecessary risk. I could probably have killed him if I had just run over. If I hadn't landed properly...

I needed to train more. Until it was no longer a risk. A predator must be competent after all.

They kept us busy. Better to avoid bullying, and why waste a second of time? We were here to win.

I kept myself more busy.

We had Sunday off, but I spent all of it training. I also spent all of the rest of the week training. I trained until my body and mind were exhausted, then threw myself back at the bench press, the weapons manual, the extra class, the firing range, the fencing strip...

How was Melody doing? She must be adapting to junior high and was probably making new friends. Did she even think of me?

I had barely time to think of her.

My parents called late one Sunday. "Ira, are you all right?" Mom asked.

"I've just been busy," I said.

"They said you had Sundays off."

"I can't talk about it." I really couldn't–the existence of the league was under NDA.

"Are you all right?"

"I'm managing," I lied.

We talked about a few more things, and when we were finished, I lay in my bed and wondered if I was cut out for this after all.

I circled the building in the air with ease.

"Good. Looks like you've figured out the hard part. Now let's make it a little harder."

Soft reds appeared in my senses. I looked and saw giant targets that floated around in the sky.

"Try to hit these while you're still flying. Don't stop, keep circling!"

I flew around and fired, fired, fired, and kept missing. "Vord," I said.

"Harder than it looks like, right?"

"How do you do this?"

"Your wetware gets you most of the way there. I wouldn't be surprised if you had to adjust it. I'll put a note in your file for the techs. But let me be frank, you're moving, the targets are moving, and eventually they'll start firing back."

I thought about that. "Let's try this again," I said.

A month after my first loss, I had not lost a single scrimmage. But I was still nervous about my next league match.

I was facing another Golem II. It couldn't be Severian, since my opponent already had a loss. It could just as well be someone else who needed the subsidy.

But a lion doesn't care about the elk's family.

His blast fired in the distance, and I followed. Then I jumped into the air and flew towards him.

Even with his wetware, he couldn't track me. I flew circles around him while he missed and missed and missed. He switched to his twin lasers but could not touch me. Then he fired ordnance into the air until he finally thought to use his drones.

I landed gently and blasted him with my power rifle. He fell over and rolled. I ran up and sliced his head off.

"YOU WON!"

I sat in my cell, exhausted. They had no victory celebration for me, but the adrenaline of victory was party enough.

I got up and looked at myself in the mirror. "I am a predator," I said.

Yes, and someone else was one life away from the end of his dreams.

Not my problem.

I took out a razor blade from my kit and scratched a tally mark on the mirror's surface. I was, after all, both warrior and weapon.

Then I went to my terminal and plugged myself in to check the standings. There were 150 three-lifers, 450 two-lifers, and 147 one-lifers. Presumably some of the one-lifers had just quit.

I checked for names. Cletus was down to one life, Priscilla was still at two, and Severian still at three.

Why did I care? They were ultimately my enemies.

But they were also the closest things I ever had to friends in this place.

I missed all my old friends, especially Melody. How were they doing? If they kicked me out, and had to return to ordinary life...

No. I wouldn't think about that.

I breathed deeply. Then I got out the calculator app and did some math. Barring some rule change, we would have ten more matches until we were just down to a handful of students. Then they would have to end the league.

I knew I could do it, even if I only had two lives.

But deep down, my heart asked what I would become.

"It's not your wetware, it's your you," the tech told me, after an unsuccessful attempt to calibrate my targeting. "Get your vording act together."

"Yes, sir," I said, irritated.

In the next training simulation, I focused on calming my emotions. The wetware could tell me probable trajectories, angles, relative positions. I listened to the data, the music of the radar, and–

I shot a target, just barely connecting.

"Just like that," Dante said. "We'll keep working on this until you can shoot them perfectly, then we'll go to them firing back."

Why would a predator change what's working? My high-speed maneuvering disoriented the other Eagle and couldn't track me before I hit him a few times.

I swooped down and got the kill.

"YOU WON!"

I breathed deeply as I woke up, savoring the adrenaline.

Even the academy's strictest rules could not prevent gossip. Four months in, I heard whisperings about Student #0625, who had won every match and every scrimmage but his first. Not even a three-lifer could say that. No one knew what Student #0625 looked like, or what his name was, but his record was indisputable.

"I heard he's the teachers' favorite," a boy whispered. "They give him special training at night."

"Like anyone could be Maximus' favorite," a girl said.

"No vording joke," another boy said.

"No, really, this place is rigged. Got to be. They focus their attention on the ones who are going to win..."

I kept quiet. I didn't care about their fear or worship. I wanted victory, and victory alone.

When I saw the next matchups, against a Harpy B numbered #0006, I froze for a moment.

I had felt nothing when Cletus was eliminated. He was too nice for this. I also felt nothing when I saw Severian win battle after battle, remaining at three lives. But Priscilla?

I had no feelings for her, but I also didn't want to cost her a life.

What did it matter? She wouldn't hesitate to take one of my lives. I downloaded the battle data and watched...

"You can't beat a Harpy in the air," Dante said, reviewing the footage with me on my insistence. I flew around in the simulation, watching like a ghost. In 'reality', the two power suits were a blur, both a neutral black. "You're too used to exploiting your one advantage. You need multiple techniques."

"Yes, sir."

One hit the ground and Priscilla's recorded self sliced him up. Then they all faded and Neo Babylon reset. Drones appeared in the sky. "These will fire back. No getting off the ground!"

"Yes, sir!" I ran as they opened fire. I shot upwards, calmly taking out one after another.

I breathed for a few seconds as they loaded us into the simulation. The Harpy B fired into the air. I deliberately waited a few seconds, then fired, myself.

I heard verniers rush with my suit-enhanced hearing. I ran towards the sound.

The Harpy unleashed a hail of drones. I calmly threw a mini-nuke and thrusted backwards. The explosion took out most of hers. I shot through the cloud of light. The blast connected. She screamed in pain.

I jumped into the air. She fired at me, knocking me away. Her drones hurried before her, harassing me.

I crashed into a building. As she blasted it to pieces, I had a moment to recover. I flew out the other end. I fired my laser, slicing through to hit her. She screamed again.

I banked around the building to find her on the ground. I fired one more time, swooped down, and ended her.

"YOU WON!"

As I woke up in the chair, I felt exhausted in more ways than one.

But elated. Nothing could stop me now.

The teachers spent more time on the survivors, now that a good chunk of the students had been eliminated.

"You nearly lost this one," Dante observed, replaying my match with Priscilla. "What gives?"

"I was lucky when she knocked me into the building."

"No, you were off your game. Normally, you don't take so many risks. What happened?"

"I... knew her."

"Ah. It happens. You have to remember that even though there's a real, living human being on the other side, you still have to win, all right?"

"All right," I said.

"Let's focus on your ordnance use. That was a good trick with your mininuke, but I've seen people just bait out all their opponent's ordnance, then rush him. You have to be careful..."

The meal times became emptier and emptier. If my reputation was growing, I didn't know about it, because soon enough each of us had a table to himself. Then multiple tables.

The food still wasn't any better.

Priscilla had been eliminated the match after mine. Severian had lost three matches in a row, and then his subsidy was no more.

I considered pouring out my water for them, but the teachers would flip: at wasting food, at connecting with my "peers", at honoring a group of losers, or all of the above.

I sighed to myself. Cletus would never have made it. Priscilla might have, if things had played out differently. Severian must have wanted to survive, not win.

All insufficient.

I was there to win.

One year after I had arrived, I was called to the principal's office after my match. Next week was graduation, and I was ranked #3.

I cared about victory, not standings. But I would have been valedictorian if it wasn't for #1 having never died and second place having one more tiebreaker point. It galled me more than I would admit.

Marcellinus Aurelius Caesar did not seem as impressive outside of a power suit. We now had identical builds, aside from his age.

He looked at me with respect. "Sit down," he ordered.

"Yes, sir," I said. I sat down.

"First and second place are out," he said without further introduction. "The nerve, after all we've spent on them."

"Sir?" I asked.

"Sex," he said. "With each other, vord it."

The thought had honestly never occurred to me, but I knew it happened. We were all under tons of stress. But a Tribune could have no attachments beyond the minimum. Anything that might give his opponent–any opponent–an edge was to be severed and systematically eradicated.

He took my silence for fellow disgust. "That makes you the valedictorian."

"Sir?" I almost couldn't breathe.

"Yes, you. You'll be the first student with only two lives to be valedictorian. You're making history."

"Yes, sir."

"I've reviewed all your matches. Admirable." He said, savoring the word. "You have become quite skilled at using your advantages to your maximum benefit. But that can make you weak as well. From this point forward, you'll be competing with other Tribune

Candidates, all of whom are as skilled or more skilled than you are. You cannot count on being better in the air. You must assume that any trick you can play has a countermeasure that your opponent knows."

"Yes, sir."

"In particular, I want to point out a flaw that this vording school puts in all of its students," the Principal said. "You don't think killing your enemy by internal injuries works. It does. But it doesn't work in the simulation."

"I was instructed to pursue the Misericord method, as it always works."

"Young man, there will come a day when you will be pulling the trigger in reality. *Will.*"

"Will," I repeated.

"I was once on the other side of this desk, hearing the same lecture. One day, you'll be on this side. Win. That's all your Tribe asks."

"Yes, sir!"

I didn't have much of a speech. Flavius Scipio Maximus's speech dwarfed it.

The Tribal Governor was a short man; not that it mattered to me, since I was already so short. His speech was long, and yet I found myself hanging on every word.

"We want peace," he began. "Your job, young men and women, is not to fight a war. The wars are over. Your job is to fight a peace. To ensure the lawful transfer of power to the next generation, and in doing so to ensure the peace and prosperity of the whole world."

This was the first time I had heard about anything but war for the last year, and as much cognitive dissonance as it caused me, I wouldn't decrease my hearing.

"We of the Blue-Gold Tribe seek not victory, but prosperity. When we reign–and all you are working as hard as possible to make us reign–Women will be free to make any choice about their own bodies, businessmen their businesses, children their educations free from religious overtones. *We* want peace. But the Violet Tribe Caucus... do not."

No one spoke, even as I turned up my hearing more.

"There will come a day when one of you will approach a Tribune from another Tribe in single combat. Maybe your enemy will be a Violet, maybe from the Violet Caucus, or maybe another Tribune from our own Alliance. I am certain it will be one of you representing our Tribe, by the skills you've shown us all yesterday. Do not turn back from your duty. It is the only way to keep the peace we have worked so hard to maintain. Thank you."

We all cheered and clapped, even the staff.

Normality

The Caesar Academy only trained Tribune Candidate Apprentices. After graduation, I was a true Tribune Candidate, and would never step foot in it again. Now, the Tribe itself would train us.

As we flew away from the complex, I felt a mixture of relief and sadness. I would miss Dante; the other teachers, not so much. But I had not only survived, I was going home as valedictorian.

When I stepped into the house, my parents hugged me, which was briefly overwhelming. I had never been touched in the last year, except one time when a teacher slapped me in the face. I tried to hug them back. "Glad... glad to be back," I stammered.

"You'll have to tell us all about it," Mom said.

What could I tell them? That I had become a predator? Did they realize I could not walk down a street without looking for threats, mines, firing angles?

"It'll be all right," Dad said. "You can just rest for now."

"Right," I said, and walked up to my room.

My room was full of old toys, paper magazines, and a bed that was the wrong size. I was horribly disoriented at first, then wanted to throw up. Detritus of a life that no longer existed.

Yet... yet deep down, I had imagined it would be waiting for me.

I walked up to the terminal in the corner and looked for the neurojack. There wasn't one.

I breathed deeply. One, two, three, four. Of course there wasn't one. Most people didn't have cybernetics in their spines.

I tapped it open like a normal person and looked at contacts. What could I tell my old friends? "I now know how to use a weapon that could destroy the whole world, but let's get together for pizza and videogames tonight?"

I saw Melody's contact in the list. Last online: five minutes ago.

I thought about it. She probably wouldn't–vord it, I wanted *someone* to talk to. I tapped her name.

Calling Melody Tanbrick Stein...

Calling Melody Tanbrick Stein...

As the call on my terminal continued to spin, I wondered if she had forgotten about me after all.

The channel opened–but no video. "Irenaeus?"

"It's me all right," I said. "How has it been?"

"Hard. I... It's been hard."

"How?"

"What's Tribune school like? Did you get to try out a power suit?"

"Not yet. But I played in a lot of simulations." I wanted to tell her everything, about how I had stopped being a kid and become a predator–but *how?* I wanted nothing more than... than for time to rewind to a year ago.

"Were you good at it?"

"I was the best. Well, third-best, but I was valedictorian after they disqualified the others for... reasons."

"I see." There was a lengthy pause.

"Melody, just tell me what's wrong, already."

"I... I caught a nanoplague."

"Melody?"

"I'm not kidding. You wouldn't recognize me. I don't have a face anymore. Thanks to the Blue-Gold's last reign, the government only pays for stabilizing treatment."

I opened my mouth to argue, but couldn't. "I'm... I'm sorry," I managed.

"It ate away ninety-nine percent of my skin. I'm... I can't stand people looking at me. I just live by myself with my parents and never leave."

"That's horrible."

"We can talk like this, but I can't do a video call, OK?"

"OK," I said. "You wouldn't recognize me either, anyway."

And so like that, we blabbered about anything we could think of.

They watched as I ate every last crumb of Mom's cake.

"Ira, are you all right?" Dad asked.

"They told us not to waste food."

"Did you have enough?" Mom asked, alarmed.

"They carefully measured it. Exactly enough calories at our activity to keep us the right size."

"Oh, honey…" Mom reached under the table and squeezed my hand–it overwhelmed me and I winced. She looked more alarmed.

I tried to think of anything to change the subject. "Dad… did you get a subsidy?"

They looked at me with confusion. "A what?"

"For me having the Tribune cybernetics."

"There was, but it didn't factor into our decision. We wanted the best life for you, and well, we thought you becoming a Tribune would be part of that."

"Oh," I said.

"Ira, what on Earth?" Mom asked. "Why even ask that?"

"They, err, wanted us to be frank." I said. How the vord would I get back to normal? Or was the door behind me shut and locked forever?

"Were there others there who needed it?" Dad asked.

"I knew one who did. He was… err, he didn't make it."

"I see," Dad said.

"Ira, dear, it's over now. Let's just calm down and relax."

I looked into her eyes, and realized for certain that I would never be normal again.

They gave us a few weeks to recover, then it was time for fitting. We went to a location unmarked on any map, where the Tribe kept the Blue-Gold power suits.

They hid it in a deep, forested valley, almost peaceful. The facility itself used cloaking technology long lost to hide itself and what it contained. Perhaps fitting, as what we were about to use was forbidden to be made again.

Power suits repaired themselves, like all the Old Technology. But every so many De-cisions, a power suit would be so badly damaged in the Final Battle that it could not be repaired. What would happen if we ran out?

After all, only one Eagle VI remained in existence.

There were one hundred twenty young men just like me who would fit perfectly inside. One by one we were fitted, and the rest of us waited in the lobby, looking at each other warily, competitors once more. We went in by achievement. As one of the valedictorians, I was third.

My hearts raced when they called my name. I walked out to the hanger, and knew, the moment I saw the Eagle VIa's sleek black form on the rack, perfectly my size, that it was mine. Almost with reverence, I put myself inside. My neurojack connected automatically.

I looked around, seeing the same familiar HUD and radar, but not in the Perfect City.

I was unnerved for a moment and unsure why. Then I saw it: The small readout on my HUD did *not* say 'SIM' in red letters.

I stood there for a few seconds, doing the ritual self-check routine. Then I stood there in thought.

What would it be like to fight in this for real?

What if–the thought entered me and did not leave–what if I just *used* this? After all, I could just fly over to Violet cities and end it early. Armed forces existed only in history books. Until they mustered another Tribune, they could not stop me.

But no.

We were civilized. Only one person needed to die for peace.

"Any problems?" the tech asked.

"No. Just... overwhelmed."

"It's your first time. Just take it easy and do a little fly around."

"All right." I ran out and jumped into the air, and flew. My brain, somehow realizing on an instinctual level that this was reality, leaped for joy. All around I saw a world that was real, not a simulated Perfect City.

I did several high-speed turns, everything working perfectly, as I really was born for this moment. Modern physics said inertia canceling was impossible; the power suit felt like nothing was more natural. Perhaps it was for the best that only the weakest weapons of the War had survived to the present.

The radar and lidar showed me a whole new world. I saw the small dot on my infrared. *C. livia domestica.* The common pigeon.

What would it be like to actually kill something?

I could resist. I was a predator, but not a monster.

But I didn't.

I pulled the trigger.

It exploded in a burst of plasma, setting fire to the tree behind it.

What had I done?

No, no, I was going to kill another human being one day. What did one small bird matter?

Yet it did.

I confessed it to Melody afterwards.

"No, you're feeling the right thing," she said. I had gotten used to the black screen, as if it was her face. "All life is sacred, or at least it's supposed to be."

"Only one person needs to die," I said. "Then everything will be all right."

Melody didn't reply.

"Melody?"

"It will be all right for *some* people."

I didn't know how to answer that.

"Whatever. Let's talk about something else."

"Let's."

After we hung up, I wondered how much artificial skin cost. Surely it didn't cost *that* much? I mentally opened the datanet, my new terminal supporting a neurojack. I could ask my parents for a share of the subsidy. They would understand, I knew. All I needed was–

14 talents?

I blinked, but the number in my mind didn't lie. No wonder Melody couldn't afford it. A new house for her body would cost as much as a new house on the street.

But *I* had artificial skin, too, right? How much did it cost to make a Tribune?

124 talents, according to estimates from publicly available Tribal budget figures.

I breathed deeply. I didn't know how much the subsidy for the parents was, but if it was even close to the amount they spent on the body of their child... No wonder Severian had fought so hard.

I pushed him out of my mind. I was glad, at least, I was not responsible for his elimination.

Still, surely we would be paid a substantial sum for success. I dialed my contact in the Tribune Affairs division.

"Irenaeus! What do you need?" the cheerful woman said.

"I was curious: how much are Tribunes paid?"

"We can get you whatever you need."

"I have a friend who was a victim of a nanoplague. Most of her skin is gone. I was wondering if you could afford to..." I saw her expression.

"Ah. That... that would be a bit much. But tell you what: if you win the Primary, we can definitely afford that for you and your friend."

"Thanks," I said.

"Is there anything else you need?"

"When do training for the Primaries begin?"

"We'll contact you in about a week. The primaries are still years off, though."

"All right," I said.

"But keep training! Is she stable—your friend?"

"Yes." At least the Blue-Gold laws paid for that. I knew that the present reign couldn't instantly undo laws enacted in the previous reign. Professor Maximus had dragged us through endless detail on how the laws were made to be at least somewhat stable. But perhaps not *all* the Violet's policies were bad.

"Then I wouldn't worry about it. You just focus on winning the Primary, and it'll all work out, all right?"

"All right," I said with relief.

When summer ended, it was back to school, sort of.

I had all the world's information at a moment's thought. I could quote from *The Wealth of Nations* just as easily as the Quran, although I did the former far more often. They did not desire me to waste any time on traditional schooling. Nor did I.

I spent almost all of my time at numerous simulation labs and training fields. Although the Primaries would take place in three years, I swore I would not lose my edge waiting for them.

Every day I trained, the same exercises over and over again until they were drilled into my soul. I would shoot, run, and fly, learning every last corner of the Perfect City. I did it so often it would seep into my dreams.

Occasionally, I would train in the actual Eagle VIa in the Nevada desert, adding new craters to the firing range. Never against another power suit, of course, but nonetheless, I memorized every last quirk that simulations could not provide. I longed for those days, rare as they were.

I also fought in simulated battles. I fought against Tribune Candidates who had graduated from other schools and even those from other Tribes in the Blue-Gold Alliance. At the Academy, I had become used to the four suits that the Blue-Gold Tribe itself had, and my inner predator was thrilled at the new challenge.

I kept winning, of course. Until one day.

Cassius was another Blue-Gold, a candidate for the Golem II. As such, we weren't really rivals. Only if things went terribly right and the Violet Caucus was so soundly defeated that only the Blue-Gold Alliance was left, and then by chance we defeated all the other allied Tribes, would two Blue-Golds ever meet in true battle.

But when you're in the simulation, none of that matters.

I heard the rumble of buildings being blown to bits the moment we fired our ready shots. I flew to a skyscraper and watched. Cassius was systematically obliterating every building in his visual field. I stayed back, wondering what his plot was.

In fact, he went around the Perfect City, blowing up everything. I decided, uncertain what he was trying to do, to stop it.

I flew into the air and charged him. He threw a mininuke. It blasted off my fields, but only barely. I banked and fired on him at a distance. He flew off and began blowing up more buildings.

What the vord?

He was a valedictorian, too, so he had to have a plan–then it hit me. No buildings meant nothing to break laserfire. And he had twice as many lasers as I did.

Geff.

I flew towards him again, and this time kept my distance. He fired back briefly, then flew by buildings. Each blast from my power rifle blew up another building.

Then he went inside one.

Easy as pie. I blasted the building's middle, so it collapsed on him. I looked for the infrared, saw it, and swooped down, Misericord drawn...

Instantly he jumped out of the rubble with his own. In a second he had sliced off my head while I had sliced through him.

"YOU LOST" appeared in my vision.

"I'd call it a draw, really," Cassius said conversationally, as we sipped coffee in the waiting room and tried to relax.

"They said you lasted a few hundred milliseconds longer."

"Yes, but if it happened in reality, the Supreme Iudices would have to rule on it. It was a draw."

I sipped my coffee. "A draw, then," I agreed.

"I'll see if I can arrange more scrimmages between us. No offense to the others, but it's hard to find a peer."

"Oh, I know what you mean," I said. "When did you think of blowing up everything?"

"I thought it up when I was watching your footage. You're good at dodging lasers, but not quite perfect."

"How about that hiding in the rubble?"

"Ah, *that?* I thought that up years ago, when I saw the last Final Battle. If you can just survive the collapse of the building, you'd certainly seem helpless enough."

"Reasonable," I said. "The only flaw is that you've only got the one element of surprise."

"But it almost worked. I take it you reacted instinctively."

"I did," I said.

"You're from Caesar's, right?"

"I am. Why?"

"They have very good reflexes, but here–" he tapped his head. "–They become rigid in their thinking. Too much indoctrination and not enough flexibility."

I was silent.

"I'm not trying to be critical. I want you to win. I want you to defeat a Violet Caucus Tribune and bring us one step closer to victory. But you have to be willing to take the steps necessary to do that."

"I agree," I said. "What do I do?"

"Take more risks, for one. You didn't even notice the times I was vulnerable, did you?"

"What?" I asked.

"Called it. You have a very cautious style, but in my academy, they gave us points for victory and nothing for survival. You take *way* too few risks, until you don't even notice when others take them."

I could feel myself flushing. "Let's go through that footage, then," I said.

From that day on, I experimented. I tried every tactic I could think of, except when the battle was being graded. Most of the tactics I tried were flawed, but a few showed promise. I iterated on them and experimented some more.

Soon enough, I was once again undefeated.

Primaries

Slowly, inevitably, the Primaries approached. At first, three years sounded like an impossible length of time, but as time ticked onwards, it became two years, then one year, until it was just a month away.

I had near-perfect grades, but that would not be enough. They put the top twenty Tribune Candidates for the Eagle VIa in a single-elimination tournament. I would only be the first seed. The winner would be the Eagle VIa Tribune Nominee, a true Tribune. The rest would simply have to adapt to civilian life.

I would be lying if I said I wasn't nervous. But I was also eager. Soon enough, I would have the money I needed to help Melody, and I would also have achieved my dreams.

Just a few more days, and I would begin.

"Enough about me. How's life for you?" I asked Melody. "I know we haven't talked in a while."

"Tiring. My... my mom wants to get me into college, somehow. We're saving up money and maybe I can get a surgery or two. If nothing else, I can wear bandages. I'm not going to let the nanoplague rule my life anymore."

"Great," I said. But inwardly, I knew something even better was in her future.

"How long do the primaries last?"

That was technically a Tribe secret, but so was that I was a Tribune Candidate. "Just two more weeks. I don't know if I'll have time during the rest of the primaries, but afterwards."

"Afterwards," she agreed.

My first match was televised to our families only–Melody didn't count. But I knew for once that Mom and Dad were seeing who I truly became.

I swore they would not see me fail.

I faced Julius, the #16th seed. (I had a bye in the first round.) He fired his ready shot the instant we loaded. I waited a few seconds, then fired mine.

As I predicted, he had lost his nerve. I saw him fly over the horizon. He unloaded all of his ordnance at once. I calmly dashed out of the way of the unguided ones and shot the drones, one at a time. He tried to flank me in the air. I controlled some of my side guns and shot at him. He dodged, but not behind a building. I fired my power rifle and hit him dead on. Then I leaped into the air, found him, fired again, swooped down, and ended him.

"YOU WON!"

As reality returned, I breathed a sigh of relief. Julius had taken way too many risks, but I had not wavered. An easy victory, perhaps.

I walked out, exhausted, to my waiting parents. They cheered and hugged me. "You did amazing!" Dad said.

I didn't tell them that half of it was that Julius was too addicted to risk-taking to win.

"You must have trained so hard for this," Mom said. "I never–I never understood."

The other family was silent, angry. They approached us. "Good game," Julius's father said, then drew a knife and charged me.

I reacted with superhuman reflexes and struck his arm and face. He fell screaming. The guards rushed in and pulled us apart.

After that, we met with our families separately, apart from those whose dreams we had destroyed.

I fought the final match of the Eagle VIa Primary against Joseph, the #2 seed. Unlike the rest of us, he was not a native Blue-Gold, and his desire to prove all our doubts wrong had driven him here.

He was also better than me in aerial combat. In the two matches we had played in scrimmages, he had nearly won twice when I tried to match him in the air.

We fired our ready shots. I decided to wait to see what he would do. So, apparently, did he.

After about twenty seconds of nothing blowing up, I decided to go on the offensive. I ran down the virtual streets in search of my target. No sign of him anywhere.

I reacted in one second and dodged as Joseph fired from a window. I fired back. He flew through the building out the other end before it collapsed. I flew after him—

—and then he was gone again.

Cunning.

This was going to take a while, wasn't it?

Six hours later, he had sniped at me from every angle, but I had not hit Joseph even once. His strategy was working. I had taken to blowing up every building that Neo Babylon had, but it was a big city, and I had to be careful not to become vulnerable while my weapons cooled down or reloaded.

As the hours progressed, I started feeling pain. I looked around carefully, then brought up my HUD.

Both of my hearts were in yellow condition: too much stress for too long. Even though this was a simulation, a Tribune's body was not designed for indefinite use.

If one or both gave out, I could be disqualified. Or I could really die.

Really die, like in the Final Battle.

Vord.

I jumped just as my radar chimed. The drone swerved and almost hit me, but crashed into a building again. I fired back and grazed Joseph's field. He flew off, and I flew after him.

He must have realized I was in bad physical condition, I knew. And a Tribune was trained to kill his opponent.

I landed and calmed my breathing. I could forcibly alter my heart rate, but that might have other side effects. On the other hand, I didn't feel like dying.

A building exploded in the distance. He must have seen my first battle with Cassius. Without buildings, I couldn't rest anywhere.

I flew over the Perfect City to a skyscraper and activated my laser. At this distance, neither my radar nor my infrared could get a lock, but I didn't need to actually *hit*.

Every time he blew up a building, I blasted back with my laser.

He must have figured it, too. He would eventually get hit. I saw him leap into the air and charge me.

I fired my power rifle and hit him dead on. He recovered and continued his charge. Vord, he still had good fields! He fired back, and I leapt into the air a second too late.

I fell, tumbling over backwards. He flew after me.

Vord it. Time to end this. I recovered, drew my Misericord and did the stupid flashy thing they told us never to do in the Academy: mid-air melee combat.

He didn't expect it. I sliced off his virtual arm. He screamed in pain and flew off.

The simulation wouldn't simulate injury to his body, other than pain. But I had damaged his fields. I just had to hunt him down now.

It wasn't hard. He had already wrecked most of the places to hide. I spotted him, fired until he stopped moving, then swooped down and ended him.

"YOU WON!"

Then I was jerked back to reality as someone forcibly unplugged me. Medical staff surrounding me immediately hurried me to a recovery room, inserting an IV in my arm as they went. I knew I was dehydrated, my hearts had almost given out, and I was mentally shot. But I had it.

I had won the Primary.

I was a Tribune Nominee.

A doctor came up to me afterwards. "You really could have died," he told me.

"I'm a Tribune Nominee, now," I said. "I might die for real."

He nodded. "But at least against a Violet."

Mom and Dad cried over me when I got home. They had a victory feast prepared, and I ate all of it without even feeling less hungry.

"We're so proud," Mom said, holding me. "You've done it. You're a Tribune."

"No matter what happens from now on," Dad said. "You've made your parents proud."

But I didn't pay attention. I had to talk to Melody.

As soon as I had eaten it all, I hurried to my room, now spartan.

Calling Melody Tanbrick Stein...

Calling Melody Tanbrick Stein...

Calling Melody Tanbrick Stein...

"Ira?" her voice came.

"I did it!" I said. "I won!"

She didn't reply.

"Melody?"

"We can't talk any more," she said.

"What? Listen, about the nanoplague–"

"Look, that was–that doesn't matter. You can't be friends with a Violet or risk your position."

I opened my mouth and closed it.

"I'm sorry. I know how much you care about the Blue-Golds. Follow their success and future, not mine." She hung up.

I mentally reached for redial, but saw her contact was blocked.

Vord!

I cried out in anger and slammed my real fist against the terminal. But what could I do? She had already blocked me.

"Afterwards," I said. When I had won, and retired.

Then I could make everything right.

Victories

My parents flew me to the Tribal Capitol once again. Though I could fly in a power suit, I still couldn't drive.

If I won, there'd be no need to ever learn.

If I lost...

No need to think about that.

The Tribal Officer was still a massive man, whom I no longer feared. I'm sure he didn't recognize me, out of the thousands and thousands of Tribune Candidate Apprentices he had once signed. "Congratulations on your victory. There is an amount of paperwork we'll have to go through."

"Of course, sir," I said.

Nothing more than the usual: swearing under penalty of perjury that I wasn't this and wasn't that, that I had told no one, that I had no attachments to a Violet or Violet Caucus citizen.

I signed it all without comment.

He pulled out an elaborate Tribal Emblem, engraved with the oldest symbols of our Tribe: the insignia of the 77th US Powered Infantry. "Place your hand on this."

I did. It felt warm to the touch.

"Repeat after me: 'I, Irenaeus Atticus Gaius, do solemnly swear on my honor and that of the whole Tribe that I will serve and uphold the Tribe, even at the cost of my life, nor will I hesitate to take the life of another.'"

"I, Irenaeus Atticus Gaius..." I repeated.

"In my authority as the duly appointed officer of the Blue-Gold Tribe, I declare you to be the Eagle VIa Tribune. Congratulations."

We shook hands. I felt emotions rush through me: pride, duty, honor, and a rainbow of similar emotions that had no names.

We met with Flavius in a private conference room, after that. All 11 of the Blue-Gold Alliance Tribunes attended.

"I don't suppose I need to tell you anything that you don't already know," Flavius said. "Let's get down to business, shall we?

"The Violet Caucus Primaries will be over in a few days. No, it's an open secret when it is. What we don't know is who their Tribunes are. But that doesn't matter, particularly.

"We have limited data on how the Violet Caucus power suits given only the censored data from the simulations, and an even smaller amount on how they perform in reality. What the Violets don't know is that we've reversed engineered a good detail of their functions from that data. After all, there are only so many new tricks they can pull.

"However, we are reasonably certain they have done the same to us. Don't expect any Tribe secret to be secret. But that's all for your information. I'm sure you'll be able to figure out their secrets better than myself.

"We will host all of you in an undisclosed location. We ask that you neither leave nor contact your family. While it would be unspeakable that the Violet Caucus would attack you outside of a sanctioned match, we cannot trust them.

"However, anything, and I mean anything, that you wish, and that will not interfere with your mission, is yours. We ask only that you focus on training and your matches.

"Any questions?"

A bulky young man, the Royal Indigo Tribune, asked, "Should we get our bucket lists done? After all..."

"The only person who's going to be dying is a Violet," Cassius said.

"A good attitude," Flavius agreed. "But to answer the question, we'd prefer if you didn't go, say, skydiving. It would be best if you could stay within the compound. But if there is something you would regret not doing, we can arrange it."

"I have a question," the Pale-Green Tribune, a young woman, asked. "What happens if we run out of the Violet Caucus?"

You could have heard a pin drop.

But Flavius was unmoved. "The structure of the tournament virtually guarantees that the Final Battle will be a Blue-Gold Alliance Tribune versus a Violet Caucus Tribune," he said. "If that is not the case, I would expect you to pursue your own Tribe's success, as you have sworn to do so. For the sake of the Blue-Gold Alliance, I humbly ask that you focus on defeating the Violet Caucus first before worrying about hypotheticals."

"Why bring this up now? We already learned all this stuff," the Harpy B Tribune said.

"Yes, and I dare say it's different if you're not a Blue-Gold," the Pale-Green Tribune said.

"Peace out, everyone," Cassius said. "There's no use fighting over it now. Regardless of who in the Blue-Gold Alliance elects the Supreme Consul, not one of us wants the Violets to win. Let's focus on that."

Agreements murmured. The Pale-Green Tribune looked mollified.

"I'll leave you all to introduce yourselves to each other," Flavius said. "I swear from the depths of my heart that I will allow the Decision to proceed as it always has. All I ask is that you focus on our true enemies first."

"Agreed," the Pale-Green Tribune said.

In the compound, we stretched out in the living room. I looked around at the eight other men and two women. These—these could be friends.

Friends to replace Melody?

"My name's Cassius," Cassius introduced himself. "I want to go on the record as not giving a vord which of us kills the Violet Tribune. You want my help, ask, and I'll do anything in my power to help you win. We're all in this together."

"Agreed," the young woman from Pale Green said. "But don't get me wrong. I'm not going to be your cannon fodder."

"No one's cannon fodder," I said. "If we got to this point, we're the best in the world at what we do."

Nods of agreement followed.

"Let's do this," grunted the Royal Indigo Tribune. "Let's kill the Violet vorder."

"Agreed," we all said.

Flavius formally introduced us to the Tribe on a recorded broadcast, in the first of many public appearances. I wore the Eagle VIa, silent as instructed, watching the studio audience look on me with awe.

Was Melody watching? Or was she focused on the Violet Tribunes?

Afterwards, we met with a seemingly endless number of important people. We couldn't shake hands–my gauntlets could crush an unprotected hand, and my fingers weren't all that mobile. They all congratulated me, cheered me on, and offered their support.

Afterwards, we watched the Violet Caucus doing the same to their twelve Tribunes. Junette O'Hara, the Violet Governor and current Supreme Consul, showered praise on them as they stood silently by. Their meet and greet followed. We stopped watching during that.

The others looked ready to fight at that very moment. But I couldn't get Melody and her words out of my mind.

I couldn't, even in scrimmages.

Cassius and I played hide-and-seek in the virtual Perfect City. The Violet had sent forth the Ophan X against Cassius, and while I couldn't pretend to be an Ophan, I could at least help practice battle against a foe with overwhelming sensory abilities.

Melody. The pain felt like it was in my heart, even if my SRS showed it at full capac–

The explosion knocked me off my feet. Cassius dived and sliced my head off.

"YOU LOST!"

I sighed as I returned to the reality of the simulation room. So much for being undefeatable. Cassius was a worthy foe, but—

Cassius walked up and shouted at me. "Get real! You call that a match?"

"I–"

"No. No excuses. That was a complete and utter failure on your part. Get your vording act together or get eliminated."

I sighed.

"Seriously, what the vord, man? You're off your game. Need to talk to someone?"

"I... It's something that you can't help me with," I said.

"Then talk to Flavius!"

"I will."

Flavius's office in our compound was spartan, except for images of the previous victorious Final Battles playing holographically on the walls. "What's the matter?"

I worked up my courage, but couldn't get enough.

"We need you on your A-game. What happened?"

I tried again, but the words wouldn't come.

"Believe me, there is nothing you can say that I have not heard before."

"My best friend is a Violet," I spat out at last. "I..."

"Ah," Flavius said, nodding sagely. "I can understand how that would put pressure on you."

"I... I failed the Tribe."

"You have not. There is nothing wrong with you having a Violet friend *afterwards*. Simply fight your hardest, and we can reunite you."

I breathed deeply. Yes. That was it.

"For the next few months, concentrate on victory. Your friend will be waiting for you. You can even tell him the full truth, after it's all over."

"Yes, sir." This had not been what I had been told earlier, but if Flavius was OK with it, I supposed I could not object. "Can I make a request for a policy change if I am the Victorious Tribune?"

"Absolutely, though I can't guarantee I can grant it."

"Restore full healthcare coverage for nanoplague victims."

"Ah. That is a tall order. But I will certainly see what I can do about it. You see, it's more complicated than simply writing a check."

Flavius went on to explain more about healthcare and in more detail than I knew there was detail to know, certainly far more than I had ever seen in datanet arguments. By the end, I didn't know if I agreed, but I knew it was more complicated than I imagined.

And yet–

And yet, as I walked back to my room, I wondered if the complexity of the situation justified a heartless response.

As much sense as he made at the time, I realized there was no going back. Would Melody and I ever have become... More? Probably not. Her parents probably wouldn't approve of a romantic relationship with a Gentile. Vord it, that didn't mean I still... I still didn't love her.

"Vord," I said out loud. "I'm losing it."

The Final Decision Tournament rules were so complicated that Professor Maximus had us go through them for literally three months. After sixty Decisions, nearly everything had been tried and new rules made to prevent it, and tradition had accumulated. The rules had reached the point where I could only understand them, not explain them to an outsider.

To make a long story short, Cassius would be first for reasons I cannot explain, fighting the Dark Blue Tribune of the Ophan X. All of us, Tribune and responsible adult alike, waited in the compound, watching a live feed of the simulation. No popcorn, no commentary, only utter concentration.

I knew I hadn't been benched, and I had gotten back on my game, but vord, *I* wanted to be first. Yet I couldn't deny that Cassius was one of the best, and being first to eliminate an enemy Tribune would aid our side immensely.

The Dark Blue Tribune was too cautious. He stood on the highest buildings in the Perfect City, sniping at Cassius occasionally. But Cassius dove into the sewers. An hour of tense boredom passed, as neither saw nor shot at the other.

Then the building exploded from the base. As the Ophan fell, Cassius leapt up and sliced him up.

We all cheered.

Our victory party was even more intense. We all ate way too much. No drugs or alcohol, but we had the most succulent of pizza. It was very good pizza.

"We're even in numbers, now," Cassius said, little moved by the party. "Still eleven to go. You're probably next, Ira."

"Really?" I asked.

"It's not tournament rules, it's morale. If we keep winning, we'll vord with their minds. You're just behind me in skill."

I was definitely ahead of Cassius in my opinion, but I nodded agreement. "To their defeat!" I said, hoisting up a can of soda.

He clinked his against mine.

Cassius was prophetic. They picked me to go next, against one of the Violet Tribunes, the Serpent IIIc. Theirs was an unorthodox matching, but allowed by the rules.

I devoured the combat data on the Serpent. It specialized in tunneling underground, the exact opposite of my own specialty. This was going to be a very long or a very short match, depending on if we tried to invade the other's favorable territory.

They drove me to the World Capitol in an unmarked, armored aircar with tinted windows. They let me down several staircases into the simulation room, this one guarded by a mixture of police from every Tribe.

I took a deep breath and attached the neurojack.

The Perfect City was no different, even if this was my first for-real match. But all the previous ones had also been real in their own ways, red SIM light or no.

I checked the SIM light one more time. The red letters were almost comforting.

We fired our ready lights. I leaped off the ground and flew to a building.

I breathed, waiting. May as well see what the Serpent would do.

It dived into the ground, according to the infrared. With all the automated cars, drones, and subways, it took my wetware a moment to pick him out.

No need to worry. How about I just blow everything up?

I leapt in the air and starting shooting up the ground. The Serpent would not get me like Cassius got the Ophan. I didn't rest on a building for longer than it took my weapons to recharge.

An hour passed, then another. I couldn't tell what the Serpent was doing, but by its infrared pattern, he was expending a huge amount of energy.

I breathed calmly and kept shooting. I was going to win this.

Then I saw the infrared moving away. Curious. I flew after him.

The world went bright as the Serpent lunged out of nowhere with mininukes. They blasted off my field. I spun out and crashed into a building, screaming in real pain. He drew his Misericord.

No.

I fired my verniers and crashed through the building behind me. He flew around and charged me. I flew away, dodging power rifle shots. He launched drones. I shot them out of the sky, then scored a direct hit.

He fell and crashed into a building.

Not falling for it. I fired, again and again, until he stopped moving. Then I swooped down and sliced him apart.

"YOU WON!"

Though I had not fought in the actual Eagle VIa, they had me wear it for the victory parade. As we passed through the streets of Chicago on a float, the crowds cheered and Blue-Gold banners flew. I fell silent, drinking it all in.

"I'm sure they'll call it luck, but that was skill," David, the Royal Indigo Tribune, said in the victory party afterwards.

"There was some luck," I admitted. I nibbled on my pizza, a bit too emotionally overwhelmed to celebrate my own victory.

"Skill. Don't be humble," David chided.

"I don't know. There's always luck," Cassius said. "If it was all skill, there'd be no reason to be careful."

"Being careful *is* part of skill."

"What the vord are you going on about?" Emily, the Pale-Green Tribune, asked. "The only thing that matters is victory."

"Victory it is, then," I said. "To victory!"

"To victory!" we all shouted.

The Spider

T hings went well after that, at first.

Violet after Violet fell in a row. They started with twelve Tribunes and with no losses on our end, they were down to six. I got used to the taste of pizza.

But as we kept winning, even the talking heads wondered what would happen if we completely annihilated the Violet Caucus.

"Watch where the vord you're going!" Emily snapped at Rachel, of the Harpy B.

"*You* watch!"

"Hold it, hold it," one of the responsible adults said. "Let's just calm down. We're all under a lot of stress right now–"

"Some people more than others," Emily spat, and walked off.

But the drama was short-lived. The Violets had their first victory.

We watched in silence as the Spider IVb blasted away at the Harpy A. Then several times more. As the screaming turned into moans, she dived and sliced apart one of the Blue-Gold Tribunes.

We had no party that week. Fatima said nothing to anyone unless it was about how to defeat the Spider.

I went up to her. "Ambushes?"

"You saw the combat data. She can disguise her infrared pattern."

I've fought against all sorts of ambushes, I didn't say. "How fast?"

She shook her head. "Faster reflexes than anyone I've ever fought, including you. She might have a different kind of wetware."

"I... see," I said.

"Or she's just more ruthless."

As if inspired by the victory, the Violet Caucus won the next two matches. Round One was down to two of us and one of them.

Emily slaughtered the Amber Tribune in a match so one-sided that even the Violet commentators remarked on it.

We really celebrated that day, and Emily actually loosened up for once. "Good ice cream," she said, stuffing herself. "Not nearly as sweet as victory."

"To victory!"

Our celebration was short-lived. The rules of the tournament did not allow byes. The Violet Caucus sent out the Spider again, against Rachel, our Harpy B.

Once again, the Spider won, leaping out of ambush with perfectly placed shots and slicing apart our Tribune.

Flavius didn't look worried, but I could tell he was. "We suspect the Spider IVb Tribune has some kind of alternate wetware. Why use her so often?"

"Right," Rachel said.

"I don't know," Cassius said. "She may just have really good reflexes. And she already beat a Harpy."

"How the vord did they make new wetware?" I asked. "The technology's long lost."

"They've had centuries to work on it and they can divert all the government funding they want," Flavius said. "But you are correct. She may simply be that good.

"But let's not worry about the *how* just yet. We need to stop her before she eliminates more of us. We have an opportunity to issue a direct challenge under Section 14c. Who wants—"

Everyone's hand shot up.

"I'm the best suited," Cassius suggested. "Toe-to-toe the Golem II has statistically better odds against the Spider IVb, and the Spider IVa back before it was destroyed. I've also been practically living in the footage."

I said nothing. The Eagle VIa would also have been a strong pick, but Cassius had a point.

"I agree," Flavius said. "Cassius, you'll be next."

We watched the battle with some trepidation. Cassius moved to the center of the city and blast vast holes in the pavement so that the Spider couldn't sneak up under him. He also blasted apart the nearby buildings, so that the Spider would not have cover.

In the middle of that, the Spider fired a mininuke from behind that blasted Cassius' fields. We almost roared as he spun, but the Spider was faster, got up and sliced his head off.

We immediately were pulled into a meeting after that.

Flavius now *definitely* looked concerned.

"She's good," Cassius said calmly. "I don't think it's wetware. I think she's just faster than anyone else."

"The Violets both deny that they are using a custom wetware and also argue that if they did it would not be illegal," Flavius said. "But here's the problem: Cassius, you were our top Tribune. That leaves Ira and Emily."

I took a deep breath.

"Why me?" Emily asked.

"You've been crushing people in scrimmages," Flavius said. "But Ira has a near-perfect record."

"You want me to challenge the Spider?" I asked.

"No. I want either or both of you to avoid the Spider as long as possible. If we can eliminate her with some other Tribune, we'll win."

"So you're benching me," I said.

"Yes. But only to protect you two."

I took a deep breath. What was I upset about? I would only have a higher chance of fighting in the Final Battle. "All right."

Round II went back and forth. Two victories, and two defeats, and the only Round II Tribunes left were Emily and I.

Once again, the Violets would have the right to make a challenge against someone from a lower round. They sent the Spider against me.

"What?" I demanded. So did Emily.

"It's too risky," Flavius said. "The optimal decision for the Blue-Gold Alliance is for Emily to intervene. The Spider can't challenge twice—"

"Oh, optimal for *you!*" Emily said. "Ira's the only true Blue-Gold left. What about the Pale Green Tribe?"

"Why are you so upset? Are you an arachnophobe?" Cassius asked.

Emily fell silent.

"If you beat her, you're one step closer to victory," I said. But inwardly I was disturbed. Maybe Emily was right—maybe there *was* some corruption.

But it didn't matter. We had to beat the Spider.

The Shark of the Pale-Green was another aerial combat power suit, and she ran literal circles around the Spider. The problem was, the Spider kept disappearing.

Emily conserved her ordnance and just focus on blasting the Spider apart. But as the hours progressed, she started moving slower and slower.

Vord, she was running out of physical health.

The Spider must have realized this too and kept prolonging the match. Emily systematically blew apart the sewers, but paused for one moment. The Spider leaped out and sliced her up.

We roared in anger.

Emily locked herself in the room after that, and we could only hear crying, screaming, and things being thrown at walls.

Flavius issued a direct challenge from the Knight IIb of the Royal Indigo to the Violet Samurai I. The Samurai I was considered one of the weakest surviving suits, but it was apparently easy to fly.

Our Tribune crushed him in any case.

Next was the Spider versus the Lion. Rafael of the Bright White had sworn he could take the Spider with ease. He was wrong.

That left four Tribunes: myself still somehow in round II, the Yellow-Red Anchor in Round III, David and the Spider in Round IV.

I almost cheered for the Spider, knowing that if she lost, I would never have a chance to face her. But I also wanted what was best for the Blue-Gold Alliance.

The Knight was slow as power suits go, and the Spider was fast. This time she made hit-and-run tactics, eventually landing a solid hit on David. Once again, she used her weapons over and over again until he was thoroughly disabled, and sliced his head off.

I did so much training after that I didn't even notice anything else. But I had to. Whoever won my next battle would go to the Final Battle. Commentators speculated on what would happen if it was the Anchor versus the Spider–perhaps we would see a Yellow-Red Supreme Consul.

But I was only faintly aware of that. It didn't matter, anyway. I knew I would win.

In my reviews of all the combat footage, I noticed the Anchor needed time to set up his drones and fortifications before he reached his full power. I just needed to attack first, and I would win.

As the simulation loaded, I breathed deeply and over again. This was no different from any other match. I was still a predator, no matter what.

The Anchor fired his ready shot.

I waited for five seconds, then another five. Then I fired mine and one second later jumped into air.

As I suspected the Anchor was caught off-guard. I tossed mininukes. He fired and shot most just out of the air. One got through.

I swerved behind and shot him with a direct hit from my power rifle. He fell over. I swooped down and ended it.

"YOU WON!"

My second victory parade was even more celebratory than the first. Everywhere banners hung and people cheered. People held up signs saying "Go Eagle!" and "Kill the Spider!"

And over and over again, I heard them chanting: "Kill the Violet! Kill the Violet! Kill the Violet!"

We had not had a victory party like this ever before. We even had a DJ. Everyone was there. Even Emily came out of her room and had some pizza.

I ate, too. This was it. I really would be in the Final Battle, and I would be the victorious Tribune.

And I would kill someone else.

It felt like a misplayed note in a symphony. So far every battle had just been simulation, but this time–

What did it matter? I had made my peace with it long ago. The Violet Tribune would equally try to kill me. It was just how the world worked. We had no other option for peace.

"You got this, man," Cassius said, clapping me on the back. "If anyone can kill that vorder, it's you."

I nodded, and bit some of the pizza. Delicious as ever.

Emily came up to me. "Did you get all of your bucket list done?"

"What?" I asked.

"Just sayin'. Fight without regrets."

"...All right," I said.

I didn't sky dive, but I did visit the War museum, I went to a concert, and I visited with my parents.

Mom couldn't stop crying over me. "My little boy, all grown up."

"It's OK, Mom," I said. "Just one more battle. I know I'll win."

Dad hugged me harder. "You can do it, Ira. You can do it."

One week before the Final Battle, after a fun-filled day before my final training began, I had a knock on my door.

The prettiest girl I had ever met let herself in.

"Who are you?" I asked.

"I'm just here to help you have a good time," she said. "You know, if there's anything left you want to do. *Anything.*"

"Did they pay you to sleep with me?" I asked.

"Nope! I volunteered," she said cheerfully. "C'mon, do you have any idea how sexy you look? You're practically made of muscle."

"Please," I said. "Leave me be."

"All right, if you insist," she said, and left me.

I groaned. I would have taken her up on it if it wasn't for Melody.

But no worries. I was almost there. One last match, and I would have everything I ever wanted.

Even her.

"Check this out," Cassius said in the simulation, and crashed through the window of a building. "If you turn down your fields, you can make it through the corridors without crashing into anything."

"That's insane," I said.

"Yeah, but there's no vording way she'll expect it. Let's practice it, just in case."

I nodded and breathed until I focused.

Tomorrow was it. The Blue-Gold Tribe had made their final challenge, demanding them to send their Tribune to face me in true combat, or forfeit to right to rule. And the Violet Tribe announced they accepted.

I spent the night alone, meditating, having made my desires clear. I was thereby quite upset when I heard a knock on the door.

I opened it to find a nondescript man handing me a nondescript envelope. "You didn't get this," he said, and left.

I locked the door and felt through the envelope. A datachip.

I knew what it had to be. Officially, this was all sorts of illegal. But could I turn it down?

Truth was, deep down, I was scared. If I vorded up, this was the End. Not of my career. Of my *me.*

I went to my terminal and looked around. No sign of anyone else. I plugged into the terminal and loaded the file.

The 3D image of a naked woman and loads of combat data immediately assaulted me. I was not so disturbed by this as the fact, downloaded into my brain, that her name was Melody Tanbrick Stein.

The Final Battle

How was this possible? Didn't I know–but it all made such horrible *sense*. Why didn't she show her face? Because she, too, had her body altered. How did she understand what it meant to be a Tribune? Because she was *too!*

Was the nanoplague story a lie from the beginning? It had to be.

I tried both to look and not look, but I could still recognize her face, altered as it was. I looked around the combat data and saw little I didn't already know.

The cloaking ability that Cassius had lost to was much less powerful than it seemed: Old Technology radiators could mask her power suit as another heat source. She must have sneaked up on all her targets simply by impersonating drones.

Someone had left a note in one corner of the datachip.

Ira,

We've found out that she *does* have a new kind of wetware, or rather an old kind. The Violets discovered a cache of Old Technology in an old firing range. They found wetware from several days into the War, far more evolved than any other surviving wetware.

If you don't win the Final Battle, the Violets will doubtlessly arrange this to be made retroactively legal. And then the Spider IVb will win every subsequent Decision.

You are our only hope.

The message was unsigned, but the words sounded like Flavius.

I sighed and unplugged. There was nothing I could do. Melody and I might have been friends—once upon a time. But now that we were both Tribunes, we could only be enemies.

I lay on the bed and set my implants to make myself sleep.

I woke up, had a nutritionally optimal breakfast, and said nothing to anyone. I put on my power suit for what could only be the final time and checked every last piece.

Flavius entered, as the did the other Blue-Gold Alliance Tribunes, even Emily. "We're all counting on you," Flavius said.

"I understand," I said. My voice was devoid of emotion.

He patted my shoulder pads. "You can do it. You'll save us all."

"I understand," I said.

I tried to meditate as they took me via aircar to the Perfect City—the real thing.

I breathed until I was calm. It was over. Or it would be when I killed her.

The aircar landed and I stepped out.

"WELCOME TO NEO BABYLON" read the sign, still unchanged after all the ages. Advertisements on billboards played, showing products long lost, made by companies that had not existed in centuries. The lights of the Perfect City were on, as they always were. The only thing that was missing was people.

The real thing was unnerving, but not nearly as unnerving as the lack of the SIM light.

"Only one of us is leaving this alive," I said. What did it matter? We hadn't even talked in a year.

Vord it. I had a job to do.

Drones flew around, watching. Unlike the simulated drones, these truly watched. Behind those drones' cameras were Flavius, Junette, all the other Tribunes, Mom and Dad, and the whole world.

In the distance, the Violet Tribune fired her ready shot.

I fired mine.

Fireworks blasted in every color–begin.

I jumped into the air and flew towards the Violet Tribune. I jinked at random. Her laser almost struck me. I launched my drones. She flew up and at me.

I fired my power rifle, hitting her directly. She screamed in pain.

"Melody!" I screamed back and cut off. She didn't, firing her own rifle and scoring a direct hit on my head. I fell, but caught myself, dialed down my fields in an instant and flew through a building.

She blasted it. I flew out the other side and fired mininukes. She wasn't ready. She shot most of them out of the air. One got through. It exploded on her.

I fired as she fell. She dodged in an instant. She flew into the ground, crashing inside the sewers.

Vord. This was going to be a long match. I hovered around and pulled the trigger on my laser. BOOM! Wait for it to cool down. Pull the trigger. BOOM!

Time passed. I could eventually destroy the whole underground, and blow up every mobile object except for the camera drones, but the sewers were extensive. I didn't know if I could take much more of this.

I had seen others lose their nerves so often that I knew I, too, would do the same if I didn't end this soon.

No, time to switch tactics. I flew down to the surface and crept towards the heat source.

"Ira? Can you hear me?" The voice echoed through the sewers.

"You know it's me?" I asked.

"Yes, you idiot, you talked all about the Eagle."

"Vord."

"Yeah."

The camera drones followed me in. Comms were jammed by both sides, except for the camera drone's frequency. What did the world think of this?

"So how did you find out?" she asked.

"I... got a datachip."

"Figured. They tried to foist one of those on me, but they didn't know I already knew."

"How hard was it to keep the secret?"

"Really vording hard. I never imagined this vordery could actually happen."

"It is pretty vorded up."

"The whole accident thing was a lie, in case you haven't figured that out."

"I did, actually."

Suddenly, her heat source winked out. Vord. Well, if she talked, I could figure out her location.

To, you know, kill her.

"Are you going to do this?" I asked.

"Yep. You?"

"It's the only way to have peace."

"Yeah."

I "looked" at my infrared. All I could see were camera drones. Would she be approaching with them?

No, idiot, she *was* one–

She jumped out of a corner with her Misericord blinding bright. She slashed my arm open. I punched her. She fell back. I fired point-blank, technology beyond human comprehension firing energies of untold destruction.

She screamed, her voice cutting through the noise.

I let go of the trigger.

The sewer had been obliterated, the sky now visible. Camera drones poured in to replace those lost.

The Violet Tribune was still there, lying in a twisted curl. Melody was still there.

Her weapons had not survived.

I hesitated.

"Are you going to kill me?" she asked.

"I have... I have to," I said.

"Get it over with, then. You've won."

"I *can't.*"

She lay there, and then coughed, a bloody, gurgling sound. "Doesn't matter. SRS is at critical and I've lost half a heart. I'm going to be dead soon enough."

"*No!*"

"Too late for that."

I knelt by her side. This was it, the greatest moment of my life, the apex of my existence as an apex predator. And I wanted nothing more than the SIM light to come back on.

Melody groaned. "This is vorded up. It all is."

"The Tribune system?"

"Yeah. It's not subtle, really. A goat for the LORD and a goat for Azazel," she said.

"What?"

"My ancestors. I didn't really believe it before now, you know." She coughed. "They would take two goats and cast lots. One to sacrifice to the LORD. One to take away the sins of the people. It never made sense to me. What the vord did the animal do? But now..." She coughed again.

"But now here we are." Camera drones hovered around us. One tried to get in the way–I ripped it out of the air and crushed it.

"We aren't really representatives, are we?" Melody asked. "We're just... the scapegoats. The human sacrifices to appease the masses."

I knelt there, silent.

"Did you actually believe any of it?"

"I did," I said. "All of it. But not anymore."

"Funny. I don't either." She coughed. "I'm dying for a cause that I don't even believe in."

"Why did you become a Tribune?"

"Did I have a choice?" She moaned. "No. No, I did."

I waited.

"Religious freedom. I knew if Flavius gets his way, they'd relegate anyone who be-lieved–" Cough. "–Anyone who believed into a nice little cage where he could pretend to believe whatever he wanted, as long as it didn't bother anyone. Shut everyone out of public life but the secularists. But in reality, the Violets don't care either, do they? It's all about power."

"I... I thought I could change the world," I said. "Make it a better place for everyone. I thought that capitalism was the best, most prosperous way to enrich everyone. I thought that women's choice was the most important thing. I didn't... I didn't want to hurt anyone."

"Heh. Maybe you're right." She gasped in pain. "Are you going to do it?"

"What?"

"Kill me, and win. You can make whatever world you want now."

"I don't want to make it without you."

"Too late."

Then I thought of it. I held my Misericord up to my neck.

"What the vord are you doing?"

"If I die, they'll have to come rescue you."

"No. Don't. I'm not going to make it. I want at least you to live."

I dropped the Misericord. Without my power suit, the sun-bright edge faded to lifeless silver.

"What would you make, if you were the Supreme Consul?" she asked.

"Anything but this."

"How would you decide who rules?"

"Voting. Or a hereditary monarchy. Anything where people don't die as... as scapegoats."

"I vote monarchy. You would make a good king."

"Maybe I would."

She breathed, painfully, slowly. "It's funny," she said at last. "I had a bucket list of things I did before this. I did them all, and they weren't enough. And now the 'afterwards' bucket is meaningless."

"So is mine."

"I don't think I realized I could die."

"Me neither. I didn't realize I would kill someone, not what that really meant."

Her breath became ragged, slower. I turned up my hearing. "Shema Yisrael... Adonai..." And then she fell silent.

My suit's datanet cache gave me what I needed. "Hear, O Israel, the LORD is our God, the LORD is One. Therefore you shall love the LORD your God with all your heart, all your soul, and all your strength," I said for her.

She didn't respond, deadly still.

"Why, God?" was my second prayer. "Why did you allow this to happen?" I slammed my gauntlet on the rubble beneath, shattering it.

No reply.

Fireworks burst in the air, bright blue and glorious gold.

The SRS replaced both my damaged arm and the crack in the power suit as I flew to the World Capitol. That was the only thing it could repair.

I saw them as dots on my infrared before I landed: Massive crowds of angry protesters, the police barely holding them at bay. A few dots watched the scene from the balcony above.

One of them was Flavius.

"Congratulations on–" he began.

I walked on, ignoring him.

"Ira–"

"You have no right to call me that!" I shouted.

He shut up.

The Supreme Iudices were waiting for me in a room full of terminals, each with a Tribal emblem. Iudex Johnson towered over me. "Have you slain your opponent?"

"I have," I said. It was true.

"Does any Tribe wish to contest this claim in battle?"

The terminals were first silent, then filled with "NO" after "NO."

"Then I declare you are the Victorious Tribune." He took the Laurel and with great ceremony put it on my helm. "I understand if you want to take a break, after, err, events, but we need to get matters done officially."

"I understand," I said. "I'm ready."

I marched into the crowded Chamber of Decision. Lawyers, politicians, even police officers watched my silent walk.

I walked up to the podium. Flavius watched me sternly, as if he could still control me. Junette watched me with hope.

I took a march-step turn, stood at the podium and faced them. The Final Ballot was before me, awaiting my signature. A pen, controlled by my brain, floated nearby, at the ready.

"Considering the circumstances," Flavius said. "I understand if you don't want to make a speech."

"Oh, I've already planned it out," I said.

They all watched me.

"You are doubtlessly all wondering if I will elect Flavius Scipio Maximus as Supreme Consul."

A lawyer spoke up. "Under section–"

"SILENCE!" I shouted, my voice magnified like a god.

Silence followed.

"The ancient Roman tribunes had the right to, with one word, condemn a piece of legislation," I said. "And that is my choice. *Veto.*" I took out my Misericord and sliced the Final Ballot in two, cutting through into the ancient podium. Then I slammed that podium with all my enhanced strength and it shattered into thousands of fragments. I ripped off the Laurel and crushed it into powdered emerald. "Find someone else to elect your vording government. I am done."

"Under section 12 of Title 1, the Victorious Tribune cannot–" the lawyer ventured again.

"Oh, shut it," Junette said. "It's over. No one will consent to your government any more, Flavius."

"You didn't win!" Flavius insisted.

"No one won," I said. "You didn't convince me to sign your vording paper. You can't convince me to sign a new one. And so you can never get my official approval to lead. Or anyone else. I am done."

"Young man–"

"I can kill everyone in this chamber if I need to. I won't. I'm tired of killing. But I can just leave." I aimed my rifle at the ceiling and with a reflexive press of the trigger blasted a hole in it. "Figure it out yourselves." I flew out.

Epilogue

The system is dead, now, long dead after ten years. Only some politicians and lawyers tried to keep it intact, but what government exists but that the people consent to it? Those who served the government, the police, the courts, the tax collectors, refused to enforce either side's putative government. And the Tribes themselves have sickened of human sacrifice.

The United Tribes are disintegrating, but slowly, gently. Every man now does what is right in his own eyes, and that is all right. Soon enough a new system will emerge, perhaps flawed, but I hope to God less bloodthirsty.

Melody is buried in the Perfect City, like all Tribunes. But the City is no longer empty. Both Blue-Gold and Violet have reprogrammed the robots to build a monument there, and schools take children to see where the old system died with her. Slowly, it's become repopulated.

They call me the Last Tribune. I've had the implants surgically removed, the nanobots extracted, and my power suit and weaponry are now collecting dust behind plexiglass in a museum in the Perfect City. I am now an ordinary individual, if a somewhat disabled one.

I thought no one could replace Melody, but time heals all wounds, even if it leaves scars. Almost nine years after the fame faded, I met a girl who understood what I went through. We married, and she's expecting our daughter.

I am going to name her Peace Melody Gaius.

The old system needed human sacrifice to continue. A human sacrifice ended it. Now all Tribes see in each other human beings, living souls too precious to sacrifice. Perhaps it will not last. Perhaps civil war will come one day, and young men and women like I will be drafted to fight in power suits. Or perhaps we have learned our lesson for good.

We haven't agreed on what the new world will be like. It may not satisfy any of us. But we can all agree to disagree now. And that is enough.

THE END

Also By

Want more dystopia? Look no further than the World of Wishes.

All you need to do get this exclusive story is sign up for my free newsletter. Just head on over to https://o-and-h-books.kit.com/032c86e136

Acknowledgments

Every hero needs a support team. I want to give a shoutout to Benjamin Cheah, Barbara Graver, Cesar Chacon, Karina Fabian, Katelin Cummins, Sarah Crickard, and Thomas Bridgeland for all their advice and help.

About Author

Matthew P. Schmidt was chosen by God in God before the existence of the world to be holy and blameless before Him. Matthew P. Schmidt is not that good at that, but he tries. He was born in Colorado Springs, Colorado, but moved at a young age to Martins Ferry, Ohio, where he lurks today.

Matthew P. Schmidt has written since he was five and dictated stories to his parents, and has programmed since he figured out how to work QBasic. He finds writing and programming to be surprisingly similarly, though admittedly typos in books do not usually cause the reader to crash. Matthew P. Schmidt is certain there are exceptions.

When not working on one of his many projects, Matthew P. Schmidt dreams of worlds that are not, in addition to much reading of books and playing of games. He enjoys the Great Blue Heron and octopuses of all kinds, no matter their plural. He often speaks of himself in the third person, and not only in online biographies. Matthew P. Schmidt attends St. Mary's Catholic Church in Martins Ferry, where he regularly eats God.

www.ingramcontent.com/pod-product-compliance
Lightning Source LLC
Chambersburg PA
CBHW022052170626
46808CB00003B/1447